Dear Parent:
Your child's love of reading starts here!

Every child learns to read in a different way and at his or her own speed. You can help your young reader improve and become more confident by encouraging his or her own interests and abilities. You can also guide your child's spiritual development by reading stories with biblical values and Bible stories, like I Can Read! books published by Zonderkidz. From books your child reads with you to the first books he or she reads alone, there are I Can Read! books for every stage of reading:

SHARED READING
Basic language, word repetition, and whimsical illustrations, ideal for sharing with your emergent reader.

BEGINNING READING
Short sentences, familiar words, and simple concepts for children eager to read on their own.

READING WITH HELP
Engaging stories, longer sentences, and language play for developing readers.

READING ALONE
Complex plots, challenging vocabulary, and high-interest topics for the independent reader.

ADVANCED READING
Short paragraphs, chapters, and exciting themes for the perfect bridge to chapter books.

I Can Read! books have introduced children to the joy of reading since 1957. Featuring award-winning authors and illustrators and a fabulous cast of beloved characters, I Can Read! books set the standard for beginning readers.

A lifetime of discovery begins with the magical words **"I Can Read!"**

Visit www.icanread.com for information on enriching your child's reading experience.
Visit www.zonderkidz.com for more Zonderkidz I Can Read! titles.

Suppose someone sees a brother or sister in need
and is able to help them. If he doesn't take pity
on them, how can the love of God be in him?
— 1 John 3:17

ZONDERKIDZ

Princess Petunia's Sweet Apple Pie
Copyright© 2011 Big Idea Entertainment, LLC. VEGGIETALES®, character names,
likenesses and other indicia are trademarks of and copyrighted by Big Idea
Entertainment, LLC. All rights reserved.
Illustrations © 2011 by Big Idea Entertainment, LLC.

Requests for information should be addressed to:

Zondervan, *Grand Rapids, Michigan 49530*

Library of Congress Cataloging-in-Publication Data

Poth, Karen
        Princess Petunia's sweet apple pie / written by Karen Poth.
            p. cm.
        Based on the video series: VeggieTales.
        ISBN 978-0-310-72162-8 (softcover)
        I. Big Idea's VeggieTales. II. Title.
    PZ7.P83975Pr 2011
    [E]—dc22.   2010028329

Editor: Mary Hassinger
Art direction: Karen Poth
Cover design: Karen Poth
Interior design: Ron Eddy

Printed in China

11 12 13 14 15 16 /SCC/ 21 20 19 18 17 16 15 14 13 12 11 10 9 8 7 6 5 4 3

I Can Read!

Princess Petunia's Sweet Apple Pie

story by Karen Poth

This is the Kingdom of Scone.

The grass is always green here.

The sky is blue.

And the air smells sweet …

like apples!

This is the Duke of Scone.

And this is Princess Petunia.

Tomorrow is a very big day
in the Kingdom of Scone!
Duke and Petunia are
hosting the Scone County Fair.

Early in the morning,
EVERYONE in Scone
will come to Duke's castle.

There will be great music,

fun games,

and Princess Petunia's

famous lemonade!

There will also be

water-skiing and

donut-tossing.

The day will end with
the King's Pie Contest.
The winner of the contest
will receive the Golden Spatula
and host the fair next year.

So today EVERYONE is baking pies.

Even mean, old Bump in the Knight

is making his famous smash apple pie!

"When I win," he grumbled,
"I'll wave my Golden Spatula
and CANCEL the
Scone County Fair."

Bump didn't like the fair.

He didn't like the noise.

He didn't really like fun!

The other knights were worried.

"We must stop Bump," they said.

"WE have to win the pie contest."

So the knights worked on their pies.

Starry Knight made a shepherd's pie.

Knight Owl made a black forest pie.

Hard Days Knight made a beetle pie.

Yuck!

Then … the knights ran

out of sugar.

"I can't make a beetle pie

without sugar,"

Hard Days Knight complained.

Petunia, Duke, and the knights

went to Bump's castle.

They asked him for some sugar.

"Go away!" Bump yelled.

He threw his pie at Duke.

Hard Days Knight got mad.

He threw his beetle pie

at Bump.

Soon all the knights were

throwing pies!

When the pie fight was over

ALL the pies were ruined.

Bump's castle was a mess.

"Don't come back!"

Bump yelled as the knights

left the castle.

Now the knights had to start over.

They all worked together

at Duke's castle.

Everyone was very tired.

At midnight, someone
knocked at the door.
It was Bump in the Knight.
What could he want?

"May I bake my pie here?"
Bump asked.

"My oven is not working."

"Go away," said all the knights.

BUT Petunia took HER pie

out of the oven.

She put Bump's in.

"God wants us to help each other,"

Petunia said.

"And Bump needs our help."

The next day at the contest,

the king picked two finalists:

Petunia's sweet apple pie

and Bump's smash apple pie.

As the king took his first bite,

he realized Petunia's pie was

not done.

Bump in the Knight won

the pie contest!

The crowd gasped as

Bump raised his Golden Spatula …

and handed it to Petunia

with a piece of smash apple pie!

"Thank you for helping me,"

Bump said with a smile.

That day, the Knights of Scone
taught Bump how to water-ski.

And Bump promised to make
next year's fair the best of all!

Suppose someone sees a brother or sister in need and is able to help them. If he doesn't take pity on them, how can the love of God be in him? — 1 John 3:17